Climb
to the
Crow's Nest

BY MARY COLEMAN JACKSON

Illustrated by
Anthony D'Adamo

FOLLETT PUBLISHING COMPANY   CHICAGO

LIBRARY OF CONGRESS CATALOG CARD NUMBER: 57-11024

Climb to the Crow's Nest

Chapter 1

Joey was sitting on his front steps trying hard to think of something interesting to do. Every now and then he threw one of the pebbles in his hand so that his dog Chappy would chase it, but this was not really fun.

All of a sudden a good idea came. He hopped up and pressed his face against the screen door with his hands on either side of his face so that he could see into the living room. "Hey, Mom!" he called, "You want me to go down to Fish Harbor and bring back some fish for dinner?"

There was a laugh in Mom's voice when she answered, "No, Joey dear. We don't want fish for dinner today. We have stuffed peppers."

"But I *want* to go to Fish Harbor," Joey said eagerly. "I like Fish Harbor. I like the boats because I want to be a fisherman. And I want to climb to the crow's nest more than anything else in the world!"

Mother smiled at Joey and used a teasing voice to say, "Don't you think you'd be afraid to climb up that ladder way up in the air and stand in that little round box at the top of the mast?"

"No!" Joey almost shouted. "Father does it all the time. He's not afraid."

Now Mom's voice was firm. "But you are just a little boy, Joey. You have to wait a little longer. You must be wise and strong to be a mastman like Father. You must have sharp eyes and steady feet for climbing to the crow's nest."

"I know it," said Joey. "And I already have sharp eyes and steady feet. I could climb to the crow's nest right now if I just had the chance."

Mother got up and came to the door. She tapped Joey's nose that was pressed so hard against the screen. "You know," she said, "I've always wanted to climb up there myself. But *I* never will and *you* must wait. Go play now. It's too bad there are no other boys in this block. But you have marbles and a tether ball and Chappy to keep you company. Go play."

She went back to her sewing machine, and Joey went back to sit on the steps. Chappy came to rub his cold nose against Joey's legs. "Poor Chappy," whispered Joey. "You're a good little dog. You needed your bath today, but Father had to go help Captain Bob get the *Sally Ann* ready for sardine season. I wish I had been awake when he left this morning. Maybe he would have taken me to help him."

This was the first Saturday in a long time that Father had not stayed at home. Joey missed him. He missed the fun they had together fixing things for Mom or walking down to Fish Harbor to look at the boats and hobnob with Father's friends. He stared into the street sulkily, but before he really

8

settled into a sulking spell, he heard a gay whistle and he saw Petey come striding down the street. Petey was one of Joey's special friends. Not to play with, of course, for Petey was a high school boy, but to talk to and worry with questions. So Joey went down to the sidewalk to wait, and when Petey came near enough, Joey caught his hand and walked along beside him. He was full of questions.

"Where you going so fast, Petey? What's your hurry?"

Petey kept walking, and his voice was joyful as he said, "I start work for Tony Petrillo today, that's what, small fry!"

"Tony Petrillo!" squeaked Joey, skipping and hopping to keep step. "Captain Tony Petrillo? How can you work for him when you are just a boy? His boat goes out and stays for months at

9

a time. You have to be a man to work for Captain
Tony."

Petey stopped and threw back his head to
laugh. "I am a man, Joey," he said. "I am sixteen
years old today. And Captain Tony is giving me a

chance on his boat." He started walking again, and Joey and Chappy kept on following.

"If you take a chance on the boat, when will you go to school?" Joey asked next. "You haven't graduated. My Dad says I have to graduate."

When Petey answered this time, his voice was not quite so friendly and happy. "Maybe I quit school, little snoopy. Maybe I need to make some money. Besides, haven't you ever heard of correspondence school?" He began walking very, very fast, so that Joey had to run to keep up.

"Don't be mad," he pleaded. "Don't be mad, Petey. I wish I could go with you. I wish I had just one chance. I bet you get to climb to the crow's nest and everything. You're lucky!"

There was a sad sound in Joey's voice that made Petey slow down and turn to look at him.

11

"So you think I'm lucky, do you?" he said. "I tell you what I'll do. Today I'm just going to look around and kinda get the feel of things. Captain Tony knows I was raised on the deck of a net boat, so a tuna clipper isn't much different. I don't think he'll mind if you come with me. So come on! But send your dog back. He'll get in the way."

Joey caught Chappy by the collar and turned him around with a shove. "Go home!" he ordered. Without looking back, he stepped up beside Petey, and the two of them began to walk again. Now that Joey was right beside him, Petey could see that his long steps were making trouble, so he reached down and took Joey's hand and helped him keep up the pace. Petey whistled, but Joey did not say a word. He was too pleased to be on his way to Fish Harbor to visit a tuna clipper.

He was so pleased that he didn't think another thought about Chappy . . . so very, very pleased that he didn't think at all about how far he had come from home without asking for permission.

Petey's way of getting to Fish Harbor was very different from the way that Joey knew. Joey had walked there many times with Father. He had ridden the bus to Fish Harbor many times with Mother when they wanted to buy fresh fish. But Petey cut across empty lots, hurried through trashy, dusty alleys, and jumped over railroad tracks or followed them a little ways. It wasn't long at all before Joey could hear Harbor sounds very clearly and smell harbor smells. He was as happy as he could be.

Suddenly car brakes screeched behind them. Petey hardly stopped at all, but Joey stood still

and looked back. Then he jerked his hand away
from Petey. "Chappy!" he called out. "What are
you doing here? Petey! Please wait. Chappy
didn't go home. He followed us!"

Petey did stop now, but when he turned, his face was ugly with a frown, and his voice was loud and cross. "Listen, small fry, I'm in a hurry. I should have left you where I found you. I can't be bothered with any old dog. Send him back if you want to go with me."

Tears began to well up in Joey's eyes. "But Petey!" he begged, "he almost got killed just now. I'll bet he doesn't even know the way back home from here."

Petey put his hand under Joey's chin and looked right into his eyes. "Listen," he said, "I don't have time to waste on that dog. And on second thought, I don't have time to waste on you. So you take that little dog and go right straight home. Scram!"

He looked such a man's look at Joey that there

was nothing for Joey to do but begin walking slowly and sadly away.

Chappy stayed close at Joey's side, and they hadn't gone very far at all when Joey realized that *he* wasn't sure about where he was and about the way to get home. He looked back to see how far away Petey was, but Petey must have turned a corner, for he was not in sight. Joey looked all around for something familiar, but everything was strange. He sat down then and pulled Chappy to the curb beside him. "Golly, Chappy," he said. "We're lost! I've got to think. Father always tells me to take time and think when I get mixed up." He could almost hear his father shouting at him. "Stand still, boy! And use your head!"

In a moment Joey had thought of a plan, and

he held Chappy still so that he could tell it to him. "Listen, Chappy," he said. "I think the best thing for us to do is to go on to Fish Harbor. I can tell that we are almost there. Then I'll find the *Sally Ann*. I know every bit of the way home from the place where the *Sally Ann* is, down all the right streets until we get to our house. Come on!"

He scrambled up, almost bumping into an old man with a cane who was walking by, and led Chappy towards Fish Harbor again.

Chapter 2

A little breeze circled about Joey as he walked along. It carried a smell of the harbor, fish, oil, and lumber, and a sweetish smell that Joey could not name. From not too far away came a loud bawling sound that was the ferryboat's landing signal. And then, down at the end of the street, Joey could see the masts and jig poles and crow's nests of fishing boats sticking up into the air. He knew that he had reached Fish Harbor.

In just a minute or two he was where he always wanted to be — close to the boats and to all the interesting sights and sounds that made Fish Harbor such a wonderful place. He looked around very carefully, for this was not the part of Fish Harbor that he knew best. It was good to be anywhere in Fish Harbor, but he needed to find the *Sally Ann.* Most of the boats here were jig boats with two long jig poles reaching above their masts and on into the sky. The others were smaller than the *Sally Ann,* with no turntable for the nets that lay tangled on the decks. And there were only one or two men to be seen with the boats. Joey was a

19

little surprised, for Fish Harbor had always seemed to be a busy place. Then he realized that these boats probably belonged to fishermen who caught other kinds of fish besides sardines — bass, mackerel, barracuda, or even tuna. The Saturday work and the excitement and fun would be near the net boats of the sardine fisherman.

Joey sighed. For a moment he wished that he had not followed Petey to Fish Harbor. He whistled to Chappy, who was nosing and pawing an old paper sack. "Here, boy," he called. "We've got to keep on walking till we find the *Sally Ann*. She's around here some place."

And they walked and walked. Joey had never known that Fish Harbor was so big. They passed boat after boat, and warehouses and a shed where some men were dipping a net into tar and then into

20

brine to set the tar. But they did not see the *Sally Ann*.

Joey began kicking at papers and cans and pieces of cork that were scattered over the wharf, and Chappy sniffed at everything Joey kicked. Then Joey began walking slower and slower. Finally he stopped. "Chappy," he called, "let's take a rest right here." They sat down together between two of the boats, and Joey let his feet swing over the side of the wharf. The water under the wharf looked heavy and brown.

"Gee, Chappy," said Joey sadly, "we never should have come so far away from home. It's going to be lunch time pretty soon, and Mother will worry." He leaned over a little and looked into the quiet water. The light from the sun cut a path into the water so that Joey could see the pilings of the

wharf reaching deeper and deeper into the water.
The slow swaying motion of the water made them
seem thin and trembly, and although Joey knew
that they were really thick and strong, he began to
feel nervous. He looked away.

He saw that he was close to the bow of the boat on his left, and he read the name aloud. *"Mary Jane!"* He thought a moment. "Hey, Chappy, that's a little bit like *Sally Ann.*" He tipped his head way back to see if the rest of the boat was like the *Sally Ann* and saw that it was only a jig boat. "Ha!" he said to Chappy. "That's just an old jig boat. It doesn't have a crow's nest. Why, two men can operate a jig boat all by themselves. I like net boats the best."

Joey closed his eyes and thought about how much he liked net boats. With their tarry-smelling nets piled on the turntable in the stern and a little net skiff sitting in a bigger net skiff way up on top of the pile. With their tall, strong masts and their long ladders leading to the crow's nest that looked like a part of a barrel. He wiggled his toes when he thought about the crow's nest, because that was the best part.

Still with his eyes closed, Joey imagined himself climbing up the ladder of steel cables and wooden crosspieces and climbing into a crow's nest. The climb would be scary and shaky, but not too much so — and how wonderful it would be to stand there, high and safe, searching the seas for sardines!

He sighed restlessly and opened his eyes. Now he looked at the boat on his right. This boat gleamed so whitely in the sun that it seemed almost new. Joey jumped up excitedly. It was a net boat, a lovely net boat, bigger and fancier than any boat he had seen so far. He stroked the smooth sides of this beautiful boat as he walked to its bow. He could not read the name painted in bright blue letters on the bow, so he whispered the letters to him-self — P-A-C-I-F-I-C M-A-I-D. He stood there quietly for a moment to admire the boat, and then it was just a fast idea and a short little downward climb, and he was standing on the deck of the boat.

Chappy didn't follow Joey right away. He whined and wagged his tail while Joey called him and whistled. But when Joey held out his arms, Chappy jumped into them like a circus dog. Joey gave him a hug for being clever and then began walking about carefully on the boat, which, for the moment, was his alone.

The swelling water beneath the boat gave it a gentle kind of sway that was pleasantly different from the steadiness of the wharf. It seemed quieter on the boat than it had on the wharf, too. Joey could hear three sounds and no more — the soft rubber padding of his sneakers against the deck, the hard little click-click of Chappy's toenails against the deck, and the flapping and chuckling of seagulls all about the boat.

"Oh, boy, Chappy!" said Joey happily. He had to jump and scramble over coiled ropes and boxes and cans that cluttered the deck of the boat, but he was having fun. He saw three black rain-coats hanging neatly on hooks outside the cabin. It made him imagine for a moment that the sea was rough and that cold high waves were plunging across the deck.

He saw a diver's suit dangling emptily from another hook. This time he imagined that he was the diver, sinking, sinking deeper and deeper in the dark water to untangle a net caught on jagged rocks.

He peered into a window and saw double-decker bunks made up neatly with blue-gray blankets. Through another window he saw a sink. A box of soap powder was sitting in the window. He pushed at the door that led in and up to the

27

wheelhouse and punched his fist into the tightness of the life preservers lashed to the wall of the cabin.

Joey walked again from bow to stern and finally stood looking out across the water. It changed from brown to gray to green as it stretched into the distance. He let his eyes travel along the breakwater which held the rough waves back so that they did not enter Fish Harbor. He stared at the lighthouse. Moaning Minnie, Father called it. Joey began to wish harder than he had ever wished anything that he could be a mastman like Father or even just have a chance on a boat, like Petey.

"Oh, Chappy," he said. "I can hardly wait until I get big!" Then he began looking at the wide, wide turntable that stretched across the stern of the boat from left to right. The dark brown net was folded on the turntable so that it was a huge pile of darkness. Big lead rings hung along the sides of the turntable, dangling from the bottom edge of the net. A little higher up, hundreds of brownish-yellowish corks were bundled together and showed where the top of the net lay in the folds. And at the highest part, far above Joey's head, there was the shape of a big gray net skiff.

"I'll bet there's even a little skiff inside the big one," Joey cried out to Chappy.

He stepped back and looked up, up, up to the crow's nest of this big boat. And as he looked, his feet began to move towards the base of one of the ladders that led to the crow's nest. His hands reached out and touched the ladder's steel cables and gripped them tightly. His knee banged into the lowest crosspiece of the ladder. And it was so good to be standing there at the bottom of the ladder that led to the crow's nest that Joey just had to climb higher and higher.

Chappy nipped at Joey's heels as they went past his nose. He put his forefeet on the lowest crosspiece, too, but when the ladder quivered just a little, he jumped back. His tail began to whip back and forth, and he began to whine. Joey did not stop climbing, and he did not look down when Chappy began trotting about excitedly. His bark came out loud and sharp, but Joey kept on climbing to the crow's nest.

While he climbed, it was easy for him to pretend that he was a mastman and that the boat was rolling with the swell of the sea's deep waves. He was more than halfway up when a loud, cross voice called his name and made him jump with surprise.

"Joey! Joey Bianco! Get down from there!"

Chapter 3

Joey hung on tightly to the cables and looked down to see the scowling face of Captain Bob turned up to him. "Get down, sir!" Captain Bob repeated. "Your dad certainly needs to tan you for trespassing on that boat. I ought to do it myself!

31

Get down. You're about ready to fall right now!"

So Joey began to come down, not like a real mastman but like a scared boy. His hands felt slippery and his feet slid off the crosspieces too quickly.

Captain Bob kept on scolding. "It's a good thing I heard that dog barking. You might have killed yourself."

Captain Bob put out his hand when Joey had climbed far enough down to be within reach, and he helped Joey to jump from the ladder back onto the wharf. Then he whistled and wheedled until Chappy jumped up onto an oilcan and he could bend way over and lift the little dog up to the wharf. He put his hand on Joey's shoulder and gave him a shake and a push. "Now then," he said. "Get home, you little rascal. I'm surprised Carla

32

let you get this far away from her!"

"I don't know the way home,' Joey said, in a soft and mumbly voice. "I'm trying to find the *Sally Ann* so I'll know the right streets."

"How did you get here, then?" Captain Bob

shouted. So Joey explained about Petey and his job and Chappy and the car that almost hit him and how he wanted to be a mastman who could climb to the crow's nest.

Captain Bob's face was more friendly after Joey finished explaining things. "So Pete Moreno's boy is taking a chance with Captain Tony," he said. "Well, that won't last long, because as soon as they take Pete's leg out of the cast, he'll make his boy go back to school!" He scratched his chin and stared down at Joey and Chappy. "You two had better follow me," he decided. "I'll take you to your father. It's time to knock off work, and he can take you home."

He began walking along the wharf with long steps that were harder for Joey to match than Petey's had been. And besides having trouble keeping step, Joey was having trouble on the inside of him. He knew that Captain Bob was right about what Father would think. He would be angry to know that Joey had come away from home without permission to climb to the crow's nest on a strange boat.

Captain Bob began to talk again. "It's a good thing I had to come down here to pay the Boat Cleaning Company. Otherwise I wouldn't have been around to hear that dog barking."

Before Joey could answer, he saw Father and the *Sally Ann.* Father was talking with the other men on the crew of the *Sally Ann,* but he stopped when he saw Captain Bob and Joey and Chappy. His eyebrows went up and his chin went down with surprise.

"Where'd you get him, Bob?" he asked his

35

captain as he came forward. "Is something wrong at home, boy?" he asked Joey.

Joey just shook his head. Captain Bob nudged him in the back. "Tell your dad where you were when I found you," he commanded.

Joey stammered and blushed and finally managed to tell his father that he had been climbing to the crow's nest on a pretty white boat with blue trimming.

"The *Pacific Maid*," said Captain Bob. He winked a strange wink at Father.

"Oh, no!" said Father, "not that boat!"

Then Father hooked his hands in his back pockets and glared at Joey. "Go sit down until I'm ready to take you home," he ordered. "I'll settle with you, that I will. Sit right on that can." He pointed to an old oilcan turned on its side. He turned his back to Joey and talked a little more to Captain Bob. After a little while he called crossly to Joey and they started home down the old familiar street that Joey knew quite well. But there was no familiar feeling, for Father did not take Joey's hand and he didn't talk about interesting things that they passed. Chappy seemed to know that things were bad, for he walked right at Joey's heels with a tired slow step.

Mother was standing on the porch when they turned the corner of the street where they lived. She was holding her hands up to her face to shield her eyes from the sun. She looked as if she had been standing there a long time. As soon as she saw Father and Joey she rushed down the steps of the porch and down to the sidewalk to meet them.

"Wherever did you find him, Joe? Where

have you been, Joey? I was nearly crazy. I was going to call the police." She said all that without stopping. Her hair wasn't combed neatly, and her apron had twisted around to one side.

Father stopped. "You mean he didn't ask you if he could come to Fish Harbor?" he roared. "Now I really am angry!" He turned to Joey and said, "Well, sir! So you think you're old enough to leave home without asking. And old enough to go prowling around on a strange boat. And old enough to climb to the crow's nest. Well, *I* don't! Not by a long shot." He stopped to take a deep breath and then went on some more. "Just for being so smart, I don't want to see you out of this yard again until I say so."

Mother looked sad when Father said this, even though she was really happy to have Joey

38

home again. "Oh, Joe," she said softly, "he was so lonesome without you! I guess he was looking for you."

Father snorted. "That's no reason to walk off from home without asking. Besides! He knows where the *Sally Ann* is berthed, and he knows where we work on our nets. He didn't need to meddle with that new fellow's boat."

Chappy wagged his tail at Father and snapped at his legs in a way that usually made Father laugh. But Father was still angry. "My mind's made up," he said. "Joey is not to leave this yard until I say so, except to go to school, or to mass, or to run an errand!" He left Mother and Joey standing there and hurried on into the house. Mother patted Joey on the shoulder and hurried behind Father to get his lunch ready, and Joey hurried around to the back yard so that no one would see him crying. Chappy hurried, too, but when he got into the yard he ran to his pan and began to drink water in a splashy way.

Now Joey sat on the *back* steps. He put his face down on his knees. He could hear his father talking in the kitchen, and the voice was still an angry one. "What kind of fisherman do you think he'll make if he doesn't learn to obey? I ought to take my belt off and tan him!"

Chapter 4

Every part of the next week was long and lonely for Joey. His school was on a hill, and from the window of his third grade room, he could look down to Fish Harbor. The men and boats were changed into toys by the distance, and it was sad for Joey to look at them and know that he could not get any closer. At home he played marbles and tether ball and tried to teach Chappy new tricks. But Chappy scampered happily out of the yard whenever he saw something interesting in the street.

All the people in the neighborhood had fishing on their minds. And the sardine fishermen were the busiest of all, for it was almost time for sardine season to begin. The men left home each morning to help prepare their netboats for fishing trips that began in the darkness and ended in the daylight, night after night during the months from October to February. There was scrubbing and cleaning and painting to be done. There were nets to mend or tar or tan, and leads and corks to be fastened to the nets. It was work for the men, and perhaps a little fun, too. It would have been fun for Joey, and perhaps a little work. But in his yard he had to stay, and he knew why. He was a lot of help to Mother, and when Father was at home, he tried to be extra good in hopes Father would change his mind. But Father didn't seem to notice.

One day at the beginning of October when Joey came home from school to eat lunch, Father was there. He was fixing the catches in the windows so that they would hold tightly, and Joey could see that he had put new latches on the front and back screen doors. He smiled when he saw Joey. "I should have waited to let you help me do this," he said, "but today was my last chance." He waited until Mother had put Joey's bowl of soup on the table and then said something else. "By the way, I guess you've had enough punishment.

You're free to leave the yard to play as long as you remember to ask your mother first." He gave Joey a long hard look and started working with the window catches again.

Joey's vegetable soup tasted better than usual, and he emptied his bowl before Mother finished making his peanut butter sandwich. While he waited he hugged himself happily, thinking of all the fun he could have after school. First he would come home to change clothes. Next he would get an apple and ask Mom if he could go to Fish Harbor. In a jiffy he would be there, right beside Father, looking and listening and helping with some of the exciting work! But Father had something else to say just as Mother put the sandwich on Joey's plate. "Well, well!" said Father, stretching his arms all the way up to the ceiling, "I've fixed

everything so the house will be safe, and now I'd
better hit the hay so I'll be fresh when the boats
go out."

Joey put his sandwich down quickly. Now *his*
eyebrows went up and his chin came down in sad

surprise. When Father went to bed at this time of day, it meant that the sardine season was on! Father would wake and eat and leave home after Joey was in bed. He would go to Fish Harbor and sail away on the *Sally Ann* with Captain Bob and Cookie, the cook, and all the other men on the crew. Joey knew that there would be no more chances for him to have fun working about the *Sally Ann* this season. Even though his punishment was over, Father would not want him hanging around the *Sally Ann* during the busy sardine days. And after the trouble with the *Pacific Maid*, Joey didn't plan to visit any other boat besides the *Sally Ann*.

Joey slipped out of his chair and picked up his coat and cap. "Good-by!" he said. "My team's up for kickball." And he hurried out of the door before Mother and Father could see how gloomy he was looking.

Sure enough, the boat went out as Joey had guessed. Before Father left home he stuck his head in the door of Joey's room and called, "See you tomorrow, Son!" But Joey was feeling sorry for himself, and he didn't want to answer. He pretended to be asleep. Before Father shut the door again he heard him say to Mother, "Be wishing for a good catch, Carla!" Then there in the dark room behind the closed door, without stopping to think, Joey did a naughty thing. He said out loud, in a slow and hateful voice, "I wish for a teensy, weensy catch. You old mean Father. You old tattletale Captain Bob. You won't let a boy have any fun. I hope you don't find not even one little skinny sardine!"

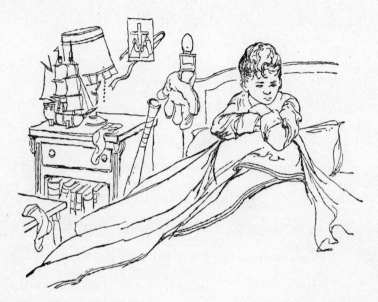

As soon as those mean words came out of
Joey's mouth and into the quiet darkness so that
Joey could hear them, he was sorry to have said
them. Even though no one else had heard the
things that he had said, Joey knew that he had
made an ugly wish, and he felt an uncomfortable
twist in his stomach.

And the terrible thing about it was this! If Mother made a wish — and she probably did — it did not come true. Not at all! The wish that came true was the hateful and ugly wish that Joey had made in his dark room while he was feeling sorry for himself!

Joey was already eating lunch when Father came home the next day. He could tell right away about the sardine catch, for Father had no smile. Mother jumped up right away and got coffee and the pipe.

"Bad luck," said Father. "Only a few tons. Too many boats in one spot, and too few sardines to go around, anyway. No boat got a good haul, and we got the smallest of all." He gulped his coffee and stretched out on the sofa without even lighting his pipe. Mother sighed wearily and hurried Joey back to school. On the way Joey couldn't help but think about the things he had wished the night before. It would be terrible, he thought, to have those things come true. He shivered.

All through October and into November, night after night the catch was small. Father and Captain Bob would talk on the telephone in the afternoon about meeting the cannery contract. Mother put the SEWING AND ALTERATIONS sign in the window as she always did when times were hard. When Joey's school had a doughnut sale, no one in the neighborhood would buy them. "We've got to save our money, Joey," they said. "The sardines aren't running so good."

Chapter 5

A feeling of worry, cold and heavy, stayed with Joey. He felt that his bad wishes had made everyone unhappy. And he was the unhappiest of all.

Then the troubles really began. Mother's

washing machine broke down, and she had to stand on the back porch and wash clean shirts for Joey and Father, even on a day when it rained and the wind blew the rain through the back porch screens. The next day she coughed and sneezed and took aspirins to help her aching throat and aching head.

When Joey came home from school, she got into bed and had Joey wash dishes and do some other housework. But she talked so weakly that Joey could hardly understand her. And Father didn't go out with the boat. He sat all night and kept the teakettle boiling out a smelly, breathy steam.

Aunt Viola came. After she made Mother's bed and washed her face and combed her hair, she whispered to Father that they should put Mother in the hospital. Aunt Viola couldn't stay to help, because her baby was too young to leave for long.

Father's voice sounded funny when he used the telephone to call the ambulance. He went next door and borrowed a little suitcase and helped Aunt Viola to put in some of Mother's things. The ambulance came quickly, and when it drove away, Father looked as if he wanted to cry. And Joey really did! Aunt Viola sniffled as she washed the dishes and made up all the beds. She kissed Joey and patted Father's back and left to catch the bus back to Torrance.

Father seemed to forget all about Joey. He walked back and forth through the house, looking in every room and staring out of every window. He didn't tell Joey to take a bath, or to eat breakfast or go to school, so Joey didn't. He followed

Father about quietly, for he was frightened and
worried, too. He had a cold, open feeling in his
stomach, and he thought he was hungry. When
Mrs. Novac, their neighbor, brought them pieces of

apple pie and cheese, Father gave him all of it, but the cold, open feeling did not go away.

That night Father looked at Joey as though he had just met him for the first time. "Boy, I forgot all about you!" he said. "Where'll you stay while I'm out with the boat?"

Joey didn't answer. He really didn't know what to say, and Mother had never wanted him to stay at home alone.

"I hate to worry the neighbors," Father went on. "They got troubles of their own. Maybe I'll take you with me. Get your things."

Joey stood still and stared.

"Hurry!" shouted Father. "Why must I tell you everything twice? I've got enough worry. Step on it!"

So Joey did get another chance to get down

to Fish Harbor and see the *Sally Ann*. It was a wonderful chance, too. For the *Sally Ann* did not sway and pull at the hawser that held her close to the wharf. Oh, no! The *Sally Ann* gave a shudder and a rumble, and her bow plowed through the black night water of Fish Harbor and her stern left white foam trails behind. The *Sally Ann* headed out the main channel of the big harbor, past Moaning Minnie, and into a sea that made her roll merrily. But the men on the boat were not happy. There were no songs and jokes and tussles like the ones Father often talked about. The men on the boat were quiet, and their faces held worried eyes and tight lips. The men were very dreary, their voices were low, but they were all very kind to Father and Joey. They kept saying over and over that they knew this night would be lucky in two ways. Carla would get better, and the sardines would run thick, hard, and fast.

"They're making good wishes for us," Joey said to himself. Their good wishes made him happy, and he began to forget about all the trouble.

But the sardines *didn't* run. There was no moon shining, and it was the kind of dark and quiet night that sardine fishermen love. The boat settled into the sea and rocked gently. Father climbed to the crow's nest and stood on the platform looking and looking for the wide ripple and glow in the water that would mean sardines. Captain Bob sat in the wheelhouse figuring on scraps of paper and then throwing the paper away. Every man was waiting and wishing for sardines. Joey was hoping for all the good wishes to make up for his bad one. But the sardines *didn't* run.

Cookie sat in the galley and played solitaire. No one called for the coffee that steamed on the stove behind him or for the thick ham sandwiches stacked on a tray on the table. Joey walked about silently, in and out of the galley, around by the turntable to look up at Father in the crow's nest, and back to the bow of the boat. Water lapped against the hull of the boat, making a dreary sound. Ropes creaked sadly, and the red and green running lights of all the other boats gleamed and shivered queerly across the water.

Suddenly Captain Bob swung out of the wheelhouse and came down on the deck where the other men stood leaning against the cabin. He called up to Father. "Come down, Joe. Let's go home. We'll start rigging for mackerel tomorrow. Fellows that don't want that, it's O.K. with me to sign on some other net boat. Sorry, but it's all I can figure out to do. We haven't cleared enough to pay for fuel so far this season."

The men just stood there. They didn't say "Yes" and they didn't say "No." And Father, who was Captain Bob's best friend, was silent, too.

Back to the wheelhouse went Captain Bob, and soon Joey could feel the boat shuddering beneath him. He knew that Captain Bob had unleashed the wheel and was turning the *Sally Ann* and heading for home. Joey wanted to cry. His foolish wish had ruined everything.

Joey didn't go with the men when Cookie yelled, "Well, you gotta live till you die, so come on and eat." Instead he stood there in the bow of the boat and was lonelier and sadder and sorrier than he had ever been in his life. Tears began to slide down his cheeks. It felt good to cry, and he blinked his eyes over and over to make the tears come faster. He wished for his mother, but Mother was sick and in the hospital. He wished for Father so that he could press his face against his rough sweater and cry out about the terrible wish that was the reason for so much trouble and sorrow. But Father had gone to eat with the crew.

Then something interested Joey so that he stopped crying. It was a kind of a funny game. He squeezed his eyes tightly together so that the tears came freely. Then he opened his eyes wide and began to stare steadily at a red light gleaming from one of the other boats that was drifting by. The tears in his eyes made the distant light shimmer and shiver and change into hundreds of tiny rainbow colored dots that seemed to float and tumble about. Joey forgot about the things that had made him cry and began squeezing his eyes shut and stretching them open as widely as possible. There he stood, squeezing and stretching until the boat that carried the light for the game had drifted too far away.

"Maybe there's another one close enough at the stern," Joey thought, and he walked back past the cabin and into the stern. Right away something in the dark water that lay endlessly behind the boat drew Joey's attention away from his game. The black water moved lazily now — all except in a place where it seemed restless and foamy. Joey watched curiously. It was not like the soapy trail the *Sally Ann* left behind as she moved through the sea. The foaminess seemed to be just beneath the surface of the water. Joey's heart began beating wildly. He stared at the restless patch in the wide dark sea. Could it be sardines? Sardines! And no man in the crow's nest to make certain?

Joey knew how important it was to be quick and sure when a school of sardines was sighted. The other boats had clever mastmen who would see them too. Or the fish might disappear as suddenly as they had come.

Joey rubbed his head nervously. He had never seen a school of sardines before. It would be terrible to get the men all excited for sardines if there were really none after all. He had to be sure — and the crow's nest was the best place to go for that. Joey started to call his father. But just then another net boat turned and began to head towards the *Sally Ann* and the part of the water where the restless foam lay. Joey knew then that the fastest way to make sure about the fish would be to climb to the crow's nest. He didn't even think of the fact that he had been forbidden to do that. He hurried towards the ladder made of steel cables that led to the small boxlike platform high above.

Chapter 6

When Joey touched the cables, they were icy, clammy cold to his hands, and the crosspieces felt thin and slippery to his feet as he stepped up. He felt a slight sway, sway as he put a hand up, a foot up, a hand up, a foot up. And as he climbed, he remembered it was forbidden, and he realized why Mother had talked about sharp eyes and steady feet and being wise and strong. Climbing to the crow's nest on a rolling swaying boat was a dangerous job. Joey was frightened, but he had to climb on. When he was as high as the roof of the cabin, he began to feel the push of a cool breeze. When he was as high as the roof of the wheelhouse, he could feel the cables bend slightly under his weight. And when he was as high above everything as he had ever been, he felt coldness, dizziness, and great waves of fear. His reaching hands brushed wood at last, and he pulled himself onto the floor of the crow's nest and stood up shakily.

He needed a moment to get his balance and catch his breath, and while he waited, clinging tightly to the narrow top of the mast, he could see

the lights of the other boats winking and bobbing,
red on the port side and green on the starboard
side.

He could see the tiny light of cigarettes burning on the dark boats riding the dark waves. Faintly he could hear the sound of voices and of radio music. He took one more deep breath and looked downward past the stern of the boat, searching the water to see if the restless foamy patches were still lying in the rolling black water. Yes! And from the height of the crow's nest the stretches of foam now seemed to be long wide ripples of silver, and the restlessness was a glowing and stirring and strange moving that could only be sardines. Sardines running thick, running hard, running fast! Closer to the *Sally Ann* than to any other boat! Joey's heart was pounding with excitement. He wanted to jump up and down and shout for joy. But unless he was quick, another boat would be first to claim the school of sardines.

Joey knelt down and began to back off the

platform, feeling about with his feet for the first crosspiece. As he did so he thought — "When I tell them about the sardines, they'll know I've climbed to the crow's nest. And I didn't exactly have permission." He moved his feet cautiously, thinking about Father's stinging belt and thinking, too, about a silly unkind wish that had almost spoiled everything. Then he began to climb down swiftly like a mastman who has been up and down the ladder many, many times. And he began to yell at the top of his voice.

"Sardines! Sardines!" He called out over and over, and when he was halfway down, Captain Bob came running.

"What are you doing up there on the ladder again?" he roared at Joey. "Get down before you fall. All we need is an accident to really put us in the red!" Then he realized what Joey was shouting, and he began to shout, too. "Sardines, men!" He stopped to look in the direction Joey pointed out to him. "A big school at last!"

The men came running quickly as Joey came down again to the deck. "Get the light on our mast," he heard his father call. "We don't want any other boat crossing our circle. These sardines are for us!"

Soon a red-beaming lantern hung high on the mast, signaling the other boats to stand clear as the *Sally Ann* put out her circle of net. The men crowded around the stern of the net boat as the winchman used the crane to tip up the nose of a little skiff that sat on the folds on the net. The skiff slid into the water, and almost before its bottom was wet, two men were jumping in. "Mola!

Mola!" the two men called from the skiff. "Mola!"
The other men echoed the word along until the
heavy net that was attached to the skiff began to
slip off the turntable where it had been stored.
First slowly and then rapidly the net went over

the stern and into the water as the *Sally Ann* hastened away.

The net skiff marked the end of the net. Captain Bob would steer his boat in a circle around the school of sardines with the net trailing off the boat and into the water. The bottom of the net would sink deep into the water pulled down by the weight of the leads strung along its edge. The top of the net would be held up by the bouncing, bobbing corks strung along its top.

Joey held his breath. Would they be able to lay the net in a circle in time to make a good catch? He didn't know how long it took, and he didn't want this school of little fish to get away.

Now Father called out, "Half the net!" The other men took up this cry. Joey saw a white ball bobbing merrily in the glistening black water. This ball marked half of the net and helped Captain Bob steer in a half circle back to the waiting net skiff. Father had told him so much about sardine fishing that Joey knew what the men would call next. And when the last fold of the net went over the stern, he helped to call out the right word — "Overboard!" The call went from man to man until Captain Bob heard it and knew the net was out. Out, that is, except for the part that was firmly attached to the turntable.

It was all very exciting, and yet the men were nearly soundless. They stood watching as though each one had the important job of steering back to the blink-blink-blink of the flashlight the men in net skiff were using to guide Captain Bob. Nearer and nearer the big boat drifted towards the skiff, dragging the net along behind. Finally the darkness no longer hid the men in the little boat, and the flashlight stopped its blinking.

The men stood back from the rail of the boat and waited in a silent moment until the skiffmen threw up the lead line of the net. "You got it?" they asked as they made the throw. "We got it!" came the answer from the *Sally Ann*. The squeaking of the winch came next as the winchman set the crane to work pulling up the lead line so that the bottom of the net would draw together and hold the fish as though they were in a basket. As the line came in, dripping water and making a swishing sound, the men began to smile, and Joey could hear, at last, a loud laugh and a snatch of a song.

The cook came next to Joey holding a lamp with a weight and a rope attached to it. When the men in the skiff called "Lamp! Lampa!" the cook

dropped the lamp over the side of the *Sally Ann,*
holding on tightly to the rope. He laughed at
Joey's surprise-open eyes. "It's a special lamp for
under water," he said.

"Why do you put it down there like that?"
asked Joey. The cook said that the net was pulled
in tightly at the bottom until it was like a bag at
the side of the boat — a big deep bag crowded
with fish. The light in the water frightened the fish
away from the open place in the side of the bag
where the two ends of the net lay between the net
skiff and the *Sally Ann.*

Everything was wonderful! Joey stepped
back from the side of the boat so that he could look
at all the men working together to bring in the fish,
his fish. "You're standing on the hatch cover," he
heard Captain Bob cry out, and then Father pulled

him out of the way as two of the men pulled at a part of the deck that opened like a trapdoor.

"We've really got a catch," Joey thought happily. He hoped it was a big one.

Two men came with a net that was hanging from a round metal rim. "The brailer," Joey said to himself. He had seen brail nets before, down at Fish Harbor when the men were dipping them into tanbark water so that they would be strong but not too stiff. The men attached the brailer to the crane, and Joey laughed, thinking that it looked like a giant's stocking cap. The crane swung the brailer out and down into the bag of fish. The crane brought the brailer up and back to the hatch loaded with swishing, flipping, twisting sardines that made a slippery slithery sound as they moved and struggled against one another. The closed end

of the brailer was tipped up. Out from the wide
open end poured the shiny, wriggly little fish,
down through the hatch into the hold of the boat.
Over and over the brail net made the trip, scooping

fish from the net in the water and pouring them into the hold. Each time the fish came tumbling out of the brailer the men's faces grew gayer, their voices grew louder, and they told another joke to anyone who would listen.

Captain Bob slapped Father on the back. "The news about this catch will help Carla to get well," he cried. "This is the largest of the season, and larger than any we took last year as well. Why, it's more than fifty tons."

Every part of Father's face took part in his smile. "The news is too good to keep," he said. "I'll try to get word to her by radio-telephone as soon as daylight comes." He winked at Captain Bob. "I'll tell her we got another mastman in the family, too. Petey Moreno isn't the only Fish Harbor boy who can help out when things are bad!"

He grinned at Joey, and Joey grinned back. The grins were proud and very happy grins.

The last brailer-load of fish had been spilled into the hold. The squeaking winch and the swaying crane began to take in the net. The leads came, clanking and clinging. The net came, high, high in the air, dripping and trickling with water and shining in the darkness because silvery fish scales were caught in its webbing. The corks came, tapping lightly against each other and looking dark brown after their soaking in the water.

"Hey, Joe! If you're waiting for daylight, you don't have long," called one of the men who had heard Father's plan to get news to Carla. As he spoke, rays of brightness fell suddenly across the sea, the boat, and the smiling men.

Seeing the sun made Joey remember that he

had been awake all night long. All in a moment he was so sleepy and tired that he didn't want to wait to see the men come aboard from the net skiff and the skiff lifted up by the crane and lowered to its place on the turntable. He yawned and stretched and rubbed his eyes.

"I'll wake you up when we pass by Moaning Minnie," called the cook as Joey stumbled into the cabin. The funny name for the lighthouse made Joey laugh drowsily. Then he heard Father say, with a teasy tone in his voice, "He'll be a Moaning Joey if I decide to get him with my belt for that climb to the crow's nest!"

All the men laughed, and Joey laughed with them. He laughed because he felt so very good inside. The feeling about the bad wish was no longer twisting about in his stomach. Mother would feel better when she heard about the big catch. Her good wish had come true. And he had climbed to the crow's nest, and Father was not *really* angry, but happy and proud.

Joey threw himself down on a bunk and went to sleep so quickly that he didn't know that Father followed him in and covered him up.